ON THE TEAM

Peter Millett   Dee Texidor

Rigby.

www.Rigby.com
1-800-531-5015

Rigby Focus Forward

This Edition © 2009 Rigby, a Harcourt Education Imprint

Published in 2007 by Nelson Australia Pty Ltd ACN: 058 280 149
A Cengage Learning company

1 2 3 4 5 6 7 8 374 14 13 12 11 10 09 08 07
Printed and bound in China

On the Team
ISBN-13   978-1-4190-3698-9
ISBN-10   1-4190-3698-X

ON THE TEAM

Peter Millett   Dee Texidor

Contents

Chapter 1

Playing Basketball

Coach Wilson said that I was not
on the school basketball team.
He said you have to pass
the ball really well
when you play basketball.

But all my friends wanted me
to be on the team.
So I showed Coach Wilson
that I really can play basketball.

On Saturday, I played for my friend
Michael's team.
One of their players was away,
so I got to fill in.

I said to Coach Wilson,
"Come and see me play."

So he did.

Chapter 2

Steals and Slam Dunks

It was a really hard game.

Coach Wilson shouted,
"Show me what you can do, Jamie!"

So I did.

A tall player was running at me
with the ball.
I took the ball right out of her hands!
The tall player was shocked.

I liked to steal the ball.
I was good at it!

"Good steal, Jamie!"
shouted Coach Wilson.

Then I moved really fast
down the court with the ball.

"Go, Jamie, go—you can do it!"
shouted Coach Wilson.

I cut to the left.
I cut to the right.

"Hey! Over here, Jamie!"
shouted Michael.

I passed the ball to Michael.

"Good play, Jamie!"
shouted Coach Wilson.

Michael ran, jumped,
and then did a slam dunk
into the hoop.
It looked really cool.

I could not slam dunk like Michael,
but I could pass the ball
and shoot hoops really well.

Now the game was really close.
Both teams were even.
We had to shoot a hoop.
We had to shoot a hoop now!

Michael passed me the ball.

"Shoot it, Jamie!"
shouted Coach Wilson.

So I cut to the left,
and I cut to the right.
Then I shot the ball at the hoop.

Chapter 3

Game Over!

The ball dropped in.

"What a shot!"
shouted Coach Wilson.

Then the game ended.
We were the winners!

Coach Wilson came over to me.

"It looks like we have a new player on the school team," he said.

"Thanks, Coach Wilson," I smiled.

How cool!
I was on the school basketball team!